Louis Shea

Noodle the CAVOODLE

Scholastic Press • New York

For Suki and the Lawson dog park gang—L.S.

Originally published in 2022 by Scholastic Australia,
an imprint of Scholastic Australia Pty Limited.

Library of Congress Cataloging-in-Publication Data Available

ISBN 978-1-5461-4083-2

10 9 8 7 6 5 4 3 2 1   24 25 26 27 28

Printed in China   127

This edition first printing, September 2024

Here's a friendly, scruffy **cavoodle**.
She has caramel fur and her name is *Noodle*.
She loves to build and paint and doodle.

But most of all she loves playing with . . .

Noodle really loves to **play**
with her friends each and every day.

On **MONDAY** she likes to **race** with Boo,
the lightning-quick Jackapoo.

TUESDAY she plays **hide-and-seek**
with the crafty Peekapoo named Zeke.

On WEDNESDAY
she plays **tug-of-war**
with the giant Great Danoodle, Thor.

THURSDAY it's time to do **cool** tricks
with Dougal the Poogle and his juggling sticks.

And on **FRIDAY** she plays a game of **catch** with the Bossi Poo brothers, Mitts, Socks, and Patch.

But SATURDAY is her favorite day because ALL her friends have come to play!

"It's great that everyone could come! TOGETHER we'll have SO MUCH FUN!"

Noodle asked, "What should we do?"

"Let's RACE each other," said the zooming Boo.

But Zeke was already hiding, just waiting for someone to find him!

Dougal had gathered
all his sticks.
He wanted the others
to watch his **tricks.**

"No, we want to play
some CATCH!"
whined the Bossi Poos,
Mitts, Socks, and Patch.

"My idea is better,"
said the Great Danoodle, Thor.
"Let's play a game of
TUG-OF-WAR!"

The pups were **cross** and not very happy.
Choosing **ONE** game had made them all **snappy**.

Her friends all **huffed** and headed home,
leaving poor Noodle all ALONE.

That night, Noodle felt quite SAD.
Her friends weren't happy. They all were mad.

"There must be something I can do
so we can all have fun **together,** too.
It's time for me to use my NOODLE!"

So she got out her book and pens to doodle.

All through the night she **worked** so hard.
And something took shape in her backyard.

She messaged her friends right away.
"Come to my house for a
SURPRISE on SUNDAY!"

Her friends came to see what Noodle had done.
And they knew right away this was going to be . . .

FUN!

There was **racing** and **hiding** and balls to **catch**,

tricks with sticks,

and a **tug-of-war** match.

But they all agreed that the very **BEST** bit . . .

... was sliding and diving into the

MUD PIT!